A Kente Dress for Kenya

by Juwanda G. Ford
Illustrated by Sylvia Walker

SCHOLASTIC INC.
New York   Toronto   London   Auckland   Sydney

ISBN 0-590-53735-0

12 11 10 9 8 7 6 5   9/9 0 1/0

Printed in the U.S.A.   24

First Scholastic printing, March 1996

It was a bright and sunny Friday morning. The students in Miss Baker's classroom sat in their chairs as the bell rang. Kenya put her notebook and pencils neatly on her desk.

Miss Baker took attendance. Then she made an important announcement.

"Our class has been selected to do a special show-and-tell program for next Friday's Parents' Night," Miss Baker said. "I would like each of you to bring in something from your favorite family activity. No live animals are allowed. Does anyone have any questions?"

Jerome raised his hand, but Kenya did not pay attention to his question. She was too busy thinking about what she could bring in for show-and-tell.

There were many family activities that Kenya enjoyed. She looked forward to family reunions at her grandfather's house every summer. She loved running through the fields playing hide-and-seek with her cousins.

She also liked the picnics she had with her parents. Sometimes, they even had them in winter. Everyone would bundle up and walk to the park. Then they would play games and have hot soup, or creamy hot chocolate, with sandwiches for lunch.

Picking one favorite family activity would not be easy for Kenya.

In the school yard during recess, everyone talked about what they were going to bring for show-and-tell. Sarah, who lived with her aunt, was excited about a special fishing pole. She and her aunt had spent a whole summer camping and learning how to fish.

Juan's family owned a restaurant, and his parents were both chefs. "I'm going to bring my special chef's hat and apron!" Juan said. "On weekends, I help my mom and dad make desserts at home."

Kenya secretly hoped that he would bring in a treat for the class!

Later in the afternoon, the class divided into groups to make decorations for Parents' Night. Kenya's group made the welcome sign. It had bright red letters, with stars pasted all around.

There was a star with each student's name. Kenya suggested that they put gold glitter around the edges of the stars. How they sparkled and twinkled!

"You are all so creative," Miss Baker said. "I can't wait to see what you bring in for show-and-tell!"

When the bell rang to end the school day, Kenya rushed out to meet her dad.

"Hi, Princess," he said. "How was school today?"

"School was great, and Miss Baker gave us a special assignment for next week's Parents' Night!"

That night during dinner, Kenya and her parents talked about the assignment. Finally Kenya made a decision.

"My favorite family activity is visiting Grandma and listening to her tell funny Anansi stories from Africa," Kenya told them.

Kenya's grandmother was a wonderful storyteller. When she performed a story, she would change her voice to sound like different characters. She would even sing or dance if it were a part of the story. And she always wore a kente cloth outfit for storytelling.

"Visiting Grandma is a great choice," Kenya's father said. "But Grandma's stories are told from her memory. There isn't anything that you could bring to show the class."

"Let's call Grandma. Maybe she can think of something," Kenya said.

Kenya dialed her grandmother's number. "Hi, Grandma! This is Kenya."

"Well, hello there, sweetie," her grandmother answered. "How's my Kenya doing today?"

"I'm okay, but I need help with my show-and-tell assignment."

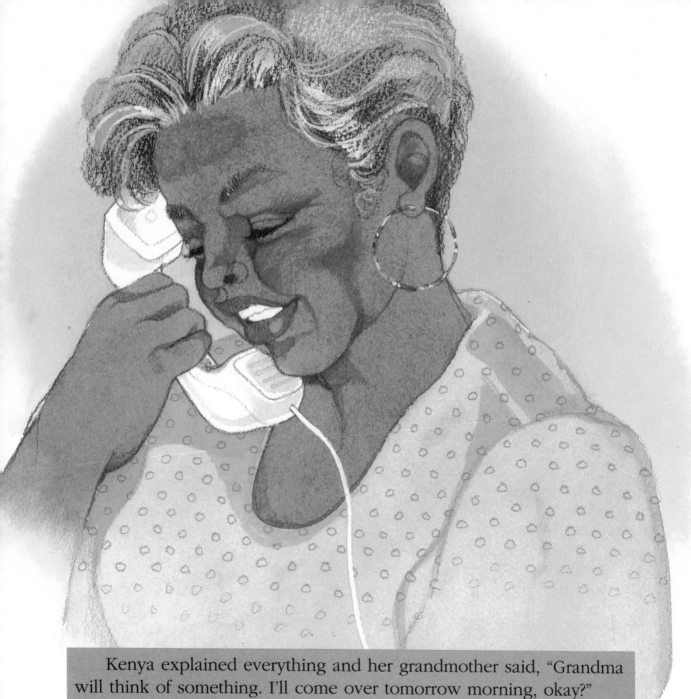

Kenya explained everything and her grandmother said, "Grandma will think of something. I'll come over tomorrow morning, okay?"
"Thank you, Grandma! I knew you would help!"

The next day, Kenya woke up early. Saturday mornings were another one of her favorite family times. She loved the fun foods her parents made. Her father's specialty was toast with smiling faces. Her mother would make pancakes filled with almost anything—fruits, nuts, and even chocolate chips! Kenya's job was to set the table.

After breakfast, Kenya went out on the porch to play with her doll and wait for her grandmother. Soon, a yellow car pulled up.

"Grandma's here! Grandma's here!" Kenya shouted.

As soon as Grandma stepped from the car, Kenya ran to hug her. Kenya's grandmother was wearing a bright green-and-yellow kente dress with a matching turban.

"Wow, Grandma! You look beautiful," Kenya said. "Is this a new storyteller's outfit?"

"Yes, it is, sweetie," her grandmother said. "As a matter of fact, this new kente cloth outfit came all the way from Ghana. Do you remember where Ghana is?"

"Ghana is in West Africa," Kenya said proudly.

Kenya took her grandmother's hand as they walked to the porch and sat on the big swing together.

"A long time ago," her grandmother continued, "only African kings and queens and their families were allowed to wear kente cloth. But now, kente cloth is made in factories all over the world, and everyone can wear it. Some people just call it kente."

"I really like it," Kenya said.

"Well, how would you like to wear a kente for show-and-tell?" her grandmother asked. "Sometimes kente cloth is used for storytelling in Africa. And most of the Anansi stories you like started in West Africa."

"Oh, Grandma, that's a great idea! It's perfect!" Kenya said.

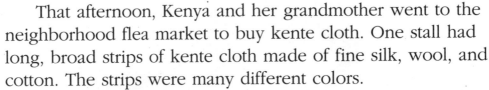

That afternoon, Kenya and her grandmother went to the neighborhood flea market to buy kente cloth. One stall had long, broad strips of kente cloth made of fine silk, wool, and cotton. The strips were many different colors.

"Now, Kenya, the colors you pick are very important," her grandmother explained. "Today, people combine colors any way they want to, but the colors of a kente cloth used to have special meanings. Gold was for riches; red and yellow were for good health; green and white were used for a good harvest; and blue symbolized a mother's love."

Kenya chose a combination of blue and gold. Her grandmother said these were also the traditional royal colors.

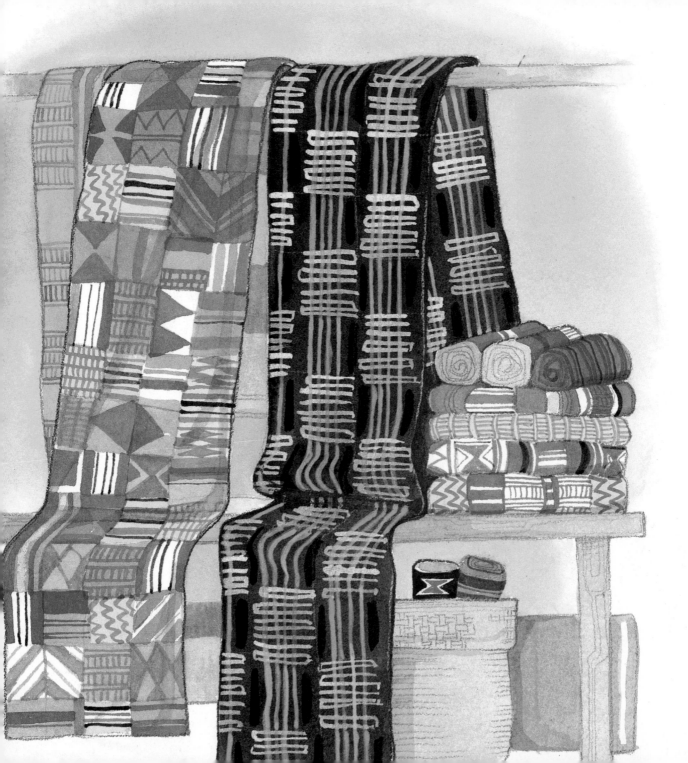

When they returned home, Kenya and her grandmother spent hours working on Kenya's kente dress. Kenya helped to cut the cloth and her grandmother sewed everything together.

As she sewed, her grandmother pointed out that certain patterns used to have different meanings, too.

"In some areas," her grandmother said, "there were even patterns made especially for some of the Anansi stories."

After they finished Kenya's outfit, they made a smaller one for Kenya's doll.

Parents' Night finally arrived. Juan was the first to make his presentation. He looked just like a chef in his tall, white hat and apron. He held up a strawberry shortcake as he talked.

Sarah was next. She explained, "The first fish I caught was a sunfish. It looked like this." She held up a fishing pole proudly. It had a paper fish on it.

Kenya looked beautiful in her kente cloth outfit. Her hair was combed in cornrows mixed with gold and blue beads.

"You look just like an African princess," her father whispered.

When it was Kenya's turn, she spoke loud and clear.

"My favorite family activity is visiting my grandmother and listening to her tell funny Anansi stories from West Africa. In the stories, Anansi the spider teaches lessons about life and about traditions.

"Tonight I am wearing a kente cloth dress. Wearing kente cloth is a tradition that started in West Africa, too. The patterns on some kente cloth were especially made for Anansi stories. . . ."

Then Kenya told her favorite Anansi story just as her grandmother had told it to her.

When Kenya finished, everyone clapped loudly, especially her grandmother, who was proudly wearing a beautiful kente, too.